P9-ELV-460

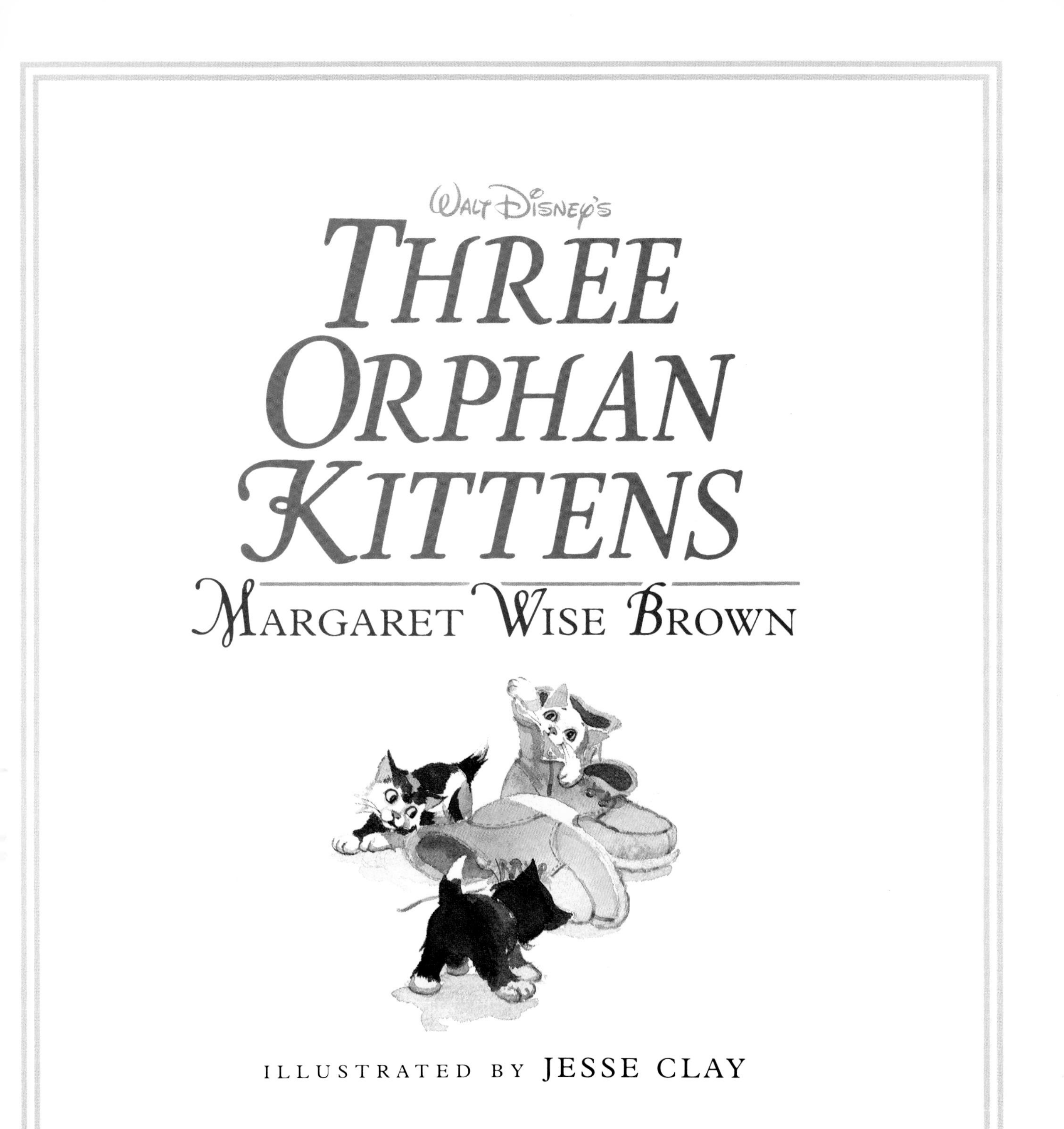

Walt Disney's

Three Orphan Kittens

Margaret Wise Brown

ILLUSTRATED BY JESSE CLAY

NEW YORK

This text originally appeared in the collection entitled
Little Pig's Picnic and Other Stories, published by D.C. Heath and Company.

Printed in the United States of America.
For information address Disney Press,
114 Fifth Avenue,
New York, New York 10011.

FIRST EDITION
1 3 5 7 9 10 8 6 4 2
Library of Congress Catalog Card Number: 94-71790
ISBN: 0-7868-3020-4/0-7868-5010-8 (lib. bdg.)

Walt Disney's

Three Orphan Kittens

Three little kittens were once born into the world. One was black. One was white. One was a calico kitten. And when they felt the warmth of their own little bodies, they all began to purr, for they thought the world was wonderful.

They even thought that the mean old farmer who owned them was wonderful. And just as soon as they could crawl, they crawled all over his house. But the farmer did not like the kittens.

"One cat on a farm is enough," the mean old farmer said to his son. "We do not have room for three more kittens."

"I know what to do," the farmer's son said. He put the three kittens in an old gunnysack. "These three little kittens will find a home if I take them into town."

The farmer's son put the gunnysack in the back of his truck and drove off. "It is cold," he said. "The kittens will be warm in the sack."

The kittens thought the old gunnysack was wonderful, too. They rolled about in the cozy darkness of the sack and wrestled and hugged each other. Then they curled up in a warm pile of fur and went to sleep.

The farmer's son hit a bump in the road. The old gunnysack flew up into the air. It came down in a soft bank of snow.

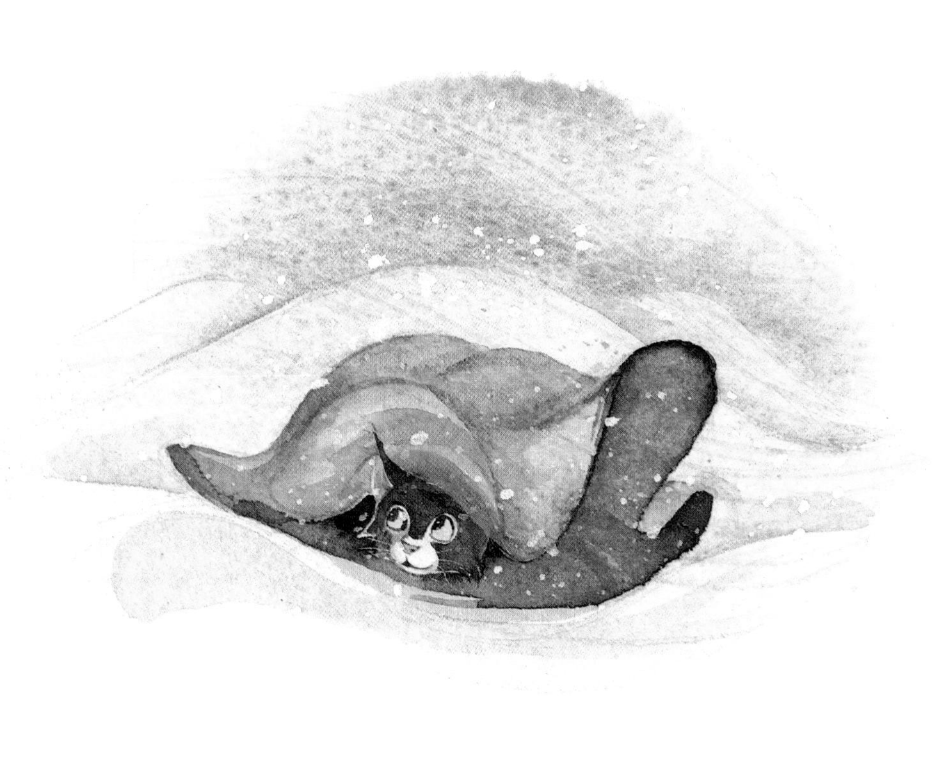

The kittens blinked open their eyes and yawned. One by one they crawled out of the old gunnysack.

They did not see the farmer's son driving away.
They did not know that they were all alone.

All that they knew was that the white snow was wonderful. They went creeping across it. Their bright little kitten eyes were shining like the stars in the night. The snow began to fall softly in the empty garden. The little black kitten batted it with his paw. And the other two kittens went pouncing after the soft snowflakes as they drifted toward the ground.

It was the little black kitten who found the cellar window open. With long leaps through the snow, the other two kittens followed him in through the open window. First they came into exciting black darkness.

The little black kitten blinked his bright yellow eyes in the darkness. The little white kitten blinked two little blue eyes, and the little calico kitten blinked his great big yellow eyes. For kittens can see in the dark.

The three little kittens crept ahead until they came to some steps. The steps were steep and hard to climb. But, one by one, each little kitten pulled himself up—step by step.

At the top of the steps was a long crack of light. Beyond was a kitchen full of good cooking smells.

Three little kitten heads came peeking through the door. And there was the most wonderful thing of all: milk! There was a full saucer of it, warm from the warmth of the room. The little kittens drank it so fast, they spattered it all over their faces.

They were sitting under the stove, licking each other clean and dry, when they heard the big feet coming. They were great big feet, the biggest feet

the kittens had ever seen. The feet came nearer. Two hands put a pie on the kitchen table. Then the feet went away.

It didn't take the three kittens long to climb right up on the table and sniff around the pie. Then the little black kitten pounced right into the middle of the pie and squirted the red juice of it into the white kitten's eye. The little calico kitten just stood on the other side of the pie and waited, with his eyes shining. And when the little black kitten crawled out of the pie and onto the table, they grabbed him. They grabbed the black kitten and gave him a good cat-scrubbing with their tongues.

Then the little black kitten went pouncing too near the edge of the tablecloth and fell. Down, down he went, pulling the whole tablecloth with him. Plates and pans came crashing down. The little white kitten slid down the tablecloth like a shoot-the-chute.

And the pie landed right on top of him. The kittens liked the noise of the crash. It was such a big, exciting noise. Then they licked themselves clean once more and went off to explore the rest of the house.

In the dining room, they saw a feather blowing about in the air. The black kitten began a dance with it. He jumped into the air and smacked the feather with his paw. The calico kitten danced, too. But it was the white kitten who discovered the hot air coming up through the grate in the floor. He put his paw in it. But the air blew right past him. He couldn't see what it was, but he knew that it was warm and soft and wonderful. He waved his paw in it back and forth, back and forth.

Then they discovered the piano. *Ping pang! Ping pang!*—kitten on the keys. The black kitten danced on the high notes, and the white kitten danced on the low notes.

At that, in came the two big feet. And the two big feet chased the three little kittens all over the house.

Finally, the kittens ran upstairs and hid in the little girl's room. They hid in her closet, and each little kitten climbed into a shoe and went to sleep.

The little black kitten climbed into a soft red slipper and went to sleep. The other two kittens climbed into a pair of sneakers and went to sleep.

There they were when the little girl found them. They were all curled up in her shoes—three sleepy little soft angel kittens. And the little girl loved them and kept them forever. And the kittens thought the little girl was wonderful. Even the cook, who owned the big feet, grew to love the three little kittens.